Michelle
the Winter Wonderland
Fairy

Special thanks to Kristin Earhart

ISBN 978-1-338-15772-7

10 9 8 7 6 5 4 3 2 1   17 18 19 20 21

Printed in the U.S.A.   40
First printing October 2017

Michelle
the Winter Wonderland
Fairy

by Daisy Meadows

SCHOLASTIC INC.

Winter is my time of year.
Why should it bring others cheer?
Why do they like the wind and snow?
This is what I want to know.

They celebrate with candles and trees.
But winter should bring them to their knees!
Only I should enjoy the chill.
And so I'll break all others' will.

I stole Michelle's magic things.
We'll see what havoc my crime brings.
No snow! No sun! No fun snow play.
Winter gloom is here to stay.

**Find the hidden letters in the stars throughout this book.
Unscramble all 9 letters to spell a special winter
wonderland word!**

The Snow Globe Search

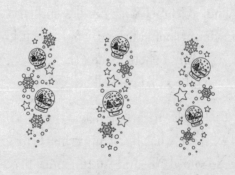

Contents

The Frosty Ferry

"It was so nice of your mom to invite me on this trip," Rachel Walker said to her best friend, Kirsty Tate. She looked out at the blue waves churning around the ferry and took a deep breath.

"The trip was my mom's prize for winning a painting contest. It was for her favorite travel website," Kirsty explained. Kirsty was proud of her mom. Mrs. Tate's oil painting was beautiful—a stunning close-up of the details of a deep green pine-tree branch, dusted with crystal-white snow. The painting's background was of the serene landscape of snow-covered hills. "I've never been to Snowbound Island before, and this is the weekend of their famous Winter Wonder Festival."

"I've never been to a winter resort, either, but the photos on the website looked almost exactly like your mom's painting," Rachel said.

"Maybe that's why she won!" Kirsty mused. "You know, my mom said she

was looking forward
to sleeping in and
having breakfast in
bed, but I'm just
excited to get
out in the snow."

"I know. We
haven't had
any snow at
home at all."
Even though it was
well into December
and almost time to celebrate the winter
holidays, the weather had been dreary
and rainy.

"My dad checked the forecast. They've
had tons of snow on the island," Kirsty said.

"I think he was right," Rachel said,
pointing.

Kirsty turned to see the sweetest tuft
of land. It looked almost like a glacier,
rising right out of the crashing waves.
From this distance, they could see the
ski slopes, treeless paths that curved
down the steep mountainside. There
was also a large, wooden building with
smoke puffing out of the chimney. Kirsty

guessed it must be the lodge. As the ferry chugged closer, the water became choppier. Rachel lost her balance, and both girls laughed as they grabbed the railing.

"I can't wait!" Rachel admitted. "I don't know if I want to ski or skate first."

"Or snowshoe or sled," Kirsty added, and then paused. "On second thought, sledding is my first choice. Definitely."

Just then, a door to the boat's cabin opened, and Mr. Tate poked his head outside. "Brrrrr," he said as the wind gusted by. "The captain said the sea is too cold and unruly, so you two need to come inside. There are huge waves and chunks of ice. It's getting dangerous."

The girls glanced out at the ocean again. The jagged ice blocks seemed to

have appeared out of nowhere, and they
were floating right in the path to the
island. The two girls took each other's
hand and carefully headed toward the
door. They had been the only ones on
the boat's deck, but the cabin was
full of people in parkas and hiking
packs.

"Did you hear that?" Kirsty whispered as soon as they entered the calm of the cabin.

"What?" Rachel wondered. "I only heard the wind and waves."

"I thought I heard some kind of bell," Kirsty explained. "Or maybe a chime. Just as we came inside."

Rachel studied her friend's face. "Really?" Rachel asked hopefully.

"Really," Kirsty confirmed, a smile twitching at the edge of her mouth.

"My fingers are crossed that you did," Rachel said, searching around for a sparkle or some other sign. Chimes, bells, and sparkles gave both girls goose bumps—and for good reason. Ever since the girls first met each other on Rainspell Island, they had been friends of the fairies. They had met all kinds of fairies. Each fairy had a special talent or interest that was connected to her own special magic. It was amazing how much the fairies did in Fairyland and the human world. Their magic inspired fun, beauty, music, kindness, and so much more.

It was also amazing how close Kirsty and Rachel had become to the fairies.

The king and queen of Fairyland now
reached out to the two girls whenever
they needed help. Because pesky Jack
Frost was always drumming up new,
evil plans, the fairies needed help quite
often. Of course, Rachel and Kirsty were
always happy to aid their fairy friends!

"Do you think Jack Frost might be up
to something?" Kirsty whispered to her
friend.

"I don't know," Rachel responded.
"But I hope he doesn't ruin your mom's
special weekend." She looked out the
window as the ferry tossed and turned
toward the dock. "It's so pretty here.
It seems especially evil for Jack Frost
and his no-good goblins to be messing
around on the island. They shouldn't
ruin everyone's chance to be in nature

and enjoy the wonders
of winter."

Kirsty giggled to
herself.

"What?" Rachel
asked.

"You sound like
you could write for
the travel website,"
Kirsty explained,
but she knew what her
best friend meant. A place like
Snowbound Island was special, and
they would do whatever they could to
make sure that her parents—and all the
guests—still had a marvelous time.

Freezing and Steaming

One of the workers from the lodge was at the dock to meet them. She had on a thick army-green coat with fake fur trim on the hood and sleeves, and a thick scarf covered her nose and mouth.

"Hi, I'm Devi," the woman said. It was hard for the girls to understand her through her chattering teeth, but her brown eyes were bright and kind. "Welcome to Snowbound Island. Let's go to the lodge." Without a smile or a nod, Devi rushed off with her hands in her pockets.

Rachel, the Tate family, and the other guests had to hurry to keep up with Devi. Each step was a struggle. The snow was deep. Kirsty was surprised by the cold. The bitter air seemed to freeze her lungs, and it made her bones hurt. They were all relieved when they reached the lodge.

The lodge was beautiful. It had sturdy wood pillars in the seating area and rich log beams in the ceiling. There was a fireplace in the center that was made of large, oval stones, and a fire snapped and crackled. Best of all, the lodge was warm.

"I've never felt cold like that before," Rachel murmured to Kirsty, her lips tinged with blue. "It didn't seem normal."

Devi overheard her. "The cold isn't normal," the guide admitted. "And it is

a surprise. The temperature dropped a
few hours ago, and it's already a record
low. The forecast said it will warm up,
so we're hopeful that we can still enjoy
many outdoor activities."

That was a relief! Kirsty and Rachel
exchanged smiles. It would be horrible to
have come all this way and not be able
to go outside and play in the snow!

"However," Devi said, "for some strange reason, there isn't enough snow on the sledding hill. So, the sledding hill is closed."

Kirsty's shoulders slumped.

"And so are the ski slopes."

Mr. Tate's shoulders slumped.

Rachel looked out the large picture window to the mountain above. From far away, it had looked like it was covered in snow. Now, she could see large muddy patches all down the slopes.

Next, she noticed a group of people dressed in tan and army green—like Devi. They were all huddled in a corner, holding clipboards and shaking their heads.

"Something's going on," Rachel whispered to Kirsty. "I don't think it's a coincidence that you heard a bell on the boat. I think something is up."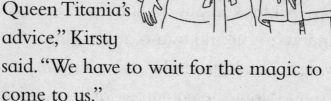

"Remember Queen Titania's advice," Kirsty said. "We have to wait for the magic to come to us."

One of the other guides rushed up to Devi and mumbled in her ear.

"And there is no ice-skating today," Devi announced, trying to force a smile as she marked something on her clipboard. "Maybe tomorrow," she added hopefully, but her forehead was all wrinkled up.

"Um, there is magic happening all around us," Rachel said. "The bad kind of magic, the kind that Jack Frost uses."

Kirsty turned to her friend. It wasn't like Rachel to make such bold statements.

"We're only here for the weekend. I want to make sure you and your family have fun, so let's keep our eyes out," Rachel said with a kind smile. "I'll bet there's something we can do."

Kirsty nodded. She was on board. Whenever they helped the fairies with a mission, they always had fun!

"Time to go to your rooms," Devi announced. "We'll come by soon to tell you about the first activity." Then Devi began to hand out keys to all the guests who had arrived on the ferry.

"This one is for you," Mr. Tate said, placing a snowflake key chain in Kirsty's hand. "We'll be right next door."

The girls unlocked their room and rushed inside. "It's perfect!" Rachel said. Cozy plaid blankets covered the beds, and the pillows had soft, flannel covers. Rachel and Kirsty's cheeks immediately turned pink from the warmth in the room.

"It's almost too cozy in here," Kirsty admitted, taking off her coat.

Rachel quickly took off hers as well.

There was a knock at the door. "It's me," called Mr. Tate. When Rachel opened it, he rushed in and headed straight for the heater by the window. He looked at the thermostat and turned the dial. Then he banged on the heating unit. "That's so weird," he said, wiping his sweaty forehead with his sleeve. "Ours is too hot, too. I'll go tell the front desk."

"Thanks, Dad," Kirsty said as her dad left the room. After he was gone, the heating unit started to make banging sounds.

"That's odd," Kirsty said, leaning closer to the metal grate. The hot rush of air made her eyes water. She blinked back

tears as she
stared into
the vent. "I'm
going to turn
this all the
way off," Kirsty
announced.

As soon as the
dial hit OFF, there
was another noise.
But this time it
sounded like the clang
of a bell. Almost immediately, a fabulous
fairy burst out of the vent, flapping
ice-blue wings that shimmered in the
afternoon light!

Wacky Winter Weather

"Thank goodness! I escaped!" the fairy exclaimed. "That heater was scorching hot!" She pulled an adorable knit hat from her head and fanned her face. "It was like an oven in there!" The fairy took a moment to catch her breath, and

the girls looked at her in awe. She wore
a turquoise coat with big buttons. Her
thick, black, curly hair came down to
her shoulders and rested on a silver scarf.
She wore high boots that almost reached
her knees—and warm knee socks that
reached even higher.

As Kirsty and Rachel watched, the
fairy pulled out her wand and whispered
a charm. At once, a burst of tiny snow
globes sprang from the wand and fell over
her like a snow shower. The fairy sighed.
"My wand has built-in air-conditioning,"
she explained with a sigh. "That's better."
The fairy placed her wand in her teeth
and held it there as she put her hat back
on her head. Then she introduced herself.
"My name is Michelle, and I am the
Winter Wonderland Fairy," she declared

with a smile. "As you might guess, I love winter!"

"We love it, too," Kirsty said to the fairy.

"I'm Rachel, and this is Kirsty," Rachel said. "We were wondering if we might meet a fairy here on the island!"

"Well, Snowbound Island is always a magical place," Michelle said. "But things are kind of wacky around here now. I'll bet you can guess why. Jack Frost is up to his old tricks. His goblins stole my three magical items—the ones that help me make winter wonderful for everyone in the human and the fairy worlds."

"Do you know where your items are?" Kirsty asked.

"Well, I suspect they are somewhere on the island. When Jack Frost zapped my items into the human world, he sent me and a bunch of his goblins, too. I ended up stuck in this heating vent. It was horrible! I think you broke Jack Frost's spell when you turned the heat all the way off. Thank you," Michelle said.

Kirsty felt herself blush. "I was happy to help. What else can we do?"

"Now I need to track down my three special objects. Will you help me?" As Michelle asked, she closed her eyes and crossed her fingers. "Pretty please?"

"Of course we will," Rachel insisted. "What are we looking for?"

"My three objects are super cool, and not just because they protect the coolest season," Michelle began to explain. "The first object is a snow globe. The snow globe makes sure there is enough snow for everyone to enjoy all the fun winter activities." Michelle then began to list all her favorite snow activities, which took a long, long time. Michelle obviously loved winter!

"The second object is a hat that looks a lot like the one I'm wearing." She pointed to her own

knit cap
with her
wand. "It has
ears, too. It
allows people
to enjoy
being outside,

even though winter can
get very chilly.

"Object number three is very special,
even though its importance is hard to
explain. It is a bright yellow candle
that I keep in a snowflake lantern.
The candle represents how the days
are shorter during winter, but also how
they begin to get longer again after
the winter solstice," Michelle said. "The
solstice is coming soon. I hope we have
the candle back by then, or some really

weird and wacky things
might happen."

"Like what?" Kirsty
asked.

"I can't be sure,"
Michelle said. "But
we should keep a
lookout for it all the
time."

Just then, there was
knocking at the door. "Quick,
Michelle, hide in my pocket!" Rachel
instructed. The fairy did just that, but
then grumbled about how hot it was.

"Hello, girls," Devi said when Kirsty
opened the door. "It's time for a sleigh
ride!"

"With real horses?" Rachel asked
hopefully.

"With real horses," Devi answered. "We'll be touring the island. There's lots to see!"

Kirsty and Rachel smiled at each other. That sounded like so much fun! The girls quickly gathered their warmest outdoor gear and hurried to the seating area in front of the lodge.

"Don't forget to put your scarf over your mouth," Mrs. Tate said to both girls as they went outside. "And cover your ears," she added, adjusting Kirsty's hood.

"We'll be fine, Mom," Kirsty assured her.

"But it is dreadfully cold," Mrs. Tate said.

"Yes, but all the sleighs have heated seats. They are very fancy," Devi told them. "Let's head outside!"

All the guests taking part in the ride headed out through the lodge's front doors.

Devi helped Mr. and Mrs. Tate into their sleigh seats. Kirsty and Rachel petted the horses while they waited.

"This is going to be the best," Kirsty said.

"There is one thing that would make it better," Rachel noted. "If it were snowing." Rachel felt a squirming from under her coat, and Michelle peeked out between two buttons.

"Find my hat, and you'll get all the snow you could wish for," she said.

"That's a deal," Rachel promised.

Sloshy Sleigh Ride

"It's so cold," Rachel said with a shiver. "I feel like my tongue could freeze."

"That's because my magic hat is missing," Michelle reminded the girls. "It makes it very hard to be outside in such frigid weather, even though we're having fun."

The girls and their new fairy friend were having fun. They were on a real sleigh ride. Real horses were pulling the sleigh! The only problem was that the sleigh path was not very snowy. The sleigh scraped over crusty ice in some places. In others, it slowed down and got stuck in sloshy mud puddles.

"I'm confused," Kirsty said. "How can there be puddles when the weather is so cold. It has to be below freezing."

"Sometimes the ground is not as cold as the air," Michelle explained, "so not all puddles freeze right away. But that's not what is happening now." Rachel and Kirsty looked over at her. "The puddles are because my magical snow globe is with the goblins. Believe it or not, the snow globe can do crazy things to winter weather if it is in the wrong hands."

"I believe you," said Kirsty. "Which of your objects should we try to track down first?"

"They are all important, so I think you should wait for the magic to come to you. Grab the first one you can find!" the fairy advised.

Michelle's plan sounded like a good one. The girls kept an eye out as the horses pulled the sleigh. The path they

followed ran along the sea, and the view
was incredible.

All at once, a gray, hazy cloud
appeared over their heads. Then, a
cold, freezing rain began to fall. "And
I thought I was cold before!" Rachel
said, her teeth chattering. The rain was
coming down so hard the girls could

barely see, and there was a furious wind
that whipped at the horses' tails.

Michelle hid under Kirsty's hood, trying
to work some magic on the dark cloud.
"My wand doesn't seem to work in this
rain," the fairy said. Her wings were wet
and limp. "I'll bet my special snow globe is
near. Remember, it can really mess up the
winter weather if it's in the wrong hands."

Kirsty and Rachel
squinted through
the heavy
drizzle, but
they couldn't
make out a
thing.

"Did you
hear that
whinny?" Rachel

said a moment later. "It sounded like
a happy horse, not a cold, soggy one."
The horses pulling their sleigh were no
longer joyfully trotting along. They were
walking slowly, carefully picking each
step along the uneven, icy path.

"Do you think there's another sleigh?"
Kirsty asked. "Maybe one traveling on a
smoother, less dangerous path?"

"Maybe a magical path?" Rachel
added, suspecting that Jack Frost's goblins
were not far off.

"There's only one way to find out!"
Michelle declared. She gave her wings a
shake and raised her wand.

What we need is a sleigh-ride gift.
With less gravity we will get a lift.
No mucky puddles or rocky ice,

Our path will now be smooth and nice.
Horses, sleigh, and passengers, too,
Will speed along for a better view.

Before the girls had time to think
about the magic charm, it began to
work. Michelle had created a tiny
sleigh pulled by two
tiny horses! With
another swish of
her wand, she
shrank the girls
and transported
them to the
new, miniature
sleigh.

Get That Globe!

The fairy-size sleigh zoomed above the trees.

"What about my parents?" Kirsty pointed out.

"Not to worry," Michelle said, "I used a special spell, so they won't notice. I hope we won't be gone long."

Another set of happy whinnies rang through the air.

"Those other horses are close," Rachel called out. "How will we find them?"

"It won't take long," Michelle announced with confidence.

The tiny horses seemed to love galloping up in the air. They sped ahead, rising and dipping along the tops of the ice-covered trees. They were small enough that they could dodge the freezing rain. But the ice was heavy. It made the limbs of the trees droop from the weight.

Before too long, the rain stopped and the wind calmed. It would have been fun if the girls weren't so worried about Michelle's snow globe. "We must be getting close," Michelle said after a while. "The weather is lovely here."

"There's snow!" Kirsty cheered. A humongous snowflake floated by. It looked like a fancy piece of lace made of ice crystals.

"And there's the other sleigh!" Rachel called out, pointing down between the evergreens.

Sure enough,
there were two
goblins in
the seat of
the sleigh.
One was
jerking the
reins to the
sleigh back

and forth. The other had both hands in
the air. He was shaking something.

"He shouldn't shake my snow globe
like that!" Michelle cried, concerned. "It
could cause a tornado. We are safe here,
so close to the globe. But the rest of the
island is in danger."

Kirsty thought of her parents on the
rough and windy path—and the steep

cliff down to the ocean.
"We have to
get your
globe now!"
Rachel
seemed deep
in thought.
"I think our best shot is if we stay
small and sneak up on them. What if we
rig a trap for the globe?"

In no time, Michelle used her magic to
make some stretchy rope. The girls tied
a velvet blanket under the sleigh, like a
pouch. "That should hold it," Rachel said,
satisfied. Next, Michelle told the horses
about their plan. Finally, it was time to act.

The tiny horses raced forward, their
mighty hooves beating through the frosty

air. They quickly caught up to the other, much larger, sleigh. Michelle flew up and landed on one of the horse's backs. "Pull up to the goblin with his hands in the air!" Michelle called out. "The one on the right." The horses nickered, agreeing with the plan. "Girls, are you ready?"

Both Rachel and Kirsty took a deep breath and gave a thumbs-up.

The horses ran even harder. Soon, they were even with the other sleigh. They snorted and pulled up, so the tiny sleigh was right next to the goblin on the right.

"Now!" Rachel and Kirsty yelled together, and they leaned out of the back of the sleigh. They both grabbed the snow globe and held on with all their might. The goblin didn't even notice them until it was too late.

"Wait! What? Stop!" the confused goblin yelled when the snow globe escaped his grasp. "Fairies! Noooooo!"

The girls dropped the heavy, oversize globe into the special velvet pouch that they had rigged.

"Now!" Michelle cried to the tiny horses. "Turn off now!"

At once,
the horses
darted
away from
the larger
sleigh. They
left the two
goblins yelling
and fighting with each
other.

Michelle flew off of the horse's back
and ducked under the velvet pouch.
When she came back out, she held the
magic snow globe. It had shrunk back
to fairy size, but the smile on Michelle's
face was gigantic. She hugged the globe
to her chest. "Thank you!" she said to
Rachel and Kirsty. "Just watch; this is
for you."

The fairy leaned down and placed a gentle kiss on the dome of the globe. Within the blink of an eye, the most gorgeous snowflakes began to fall. They were big and lush—perfect for sledding, skiing, and sleigh riding.

The heavy ice that had been on the trees was now gone. Instead, there was a light dusting of snow. They looked like the trees in Mrs. Tate's painting again.

"I need to get this snow globe back to Fairyland," Michelle said. "But first I'll return you to your sleigh." Michelle raised her wand, and a cloud of glitter burst around her and the girls. In a blink, they were back to their original size, sitting behind Kirsty's parents in the sleigh.

"The rest of your sleigh ride should be as smooth as silk," Michelle told them. "Or maybe I should say 'as smooth as magical snow.'" Michelle giggled and raised her wand again. Suddenly, each snowflake seemed to sparkle. "This will be one sleigh ride you will never forget," she said with a smile. "And don't forget to look for my other two objects!" Without another word, the fairy was gone.

"I hope all of the activities on Snowbound Island are as memorable as this ride," Rachel said, snuggling under a blanket that the guides had just pulled out. "But it's still cold."

"And it seems early for the stars to be coming out," Kirsty added with a shiver as she looked up at the darkening sky.

"That's because we still have magic objects to find," Rachel realized. "I can't wait to see which magical item we stumble upon next!"

Hot on the Hat Trail

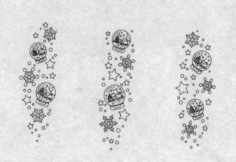

Contents

Bitter Bitterness

A hazy light came in through the
windows, telling the girls it was morning.
It was time to wake up and enjoy
Snowbound Island! But the girls didn't
move.

"Chilly, chilly, chilly," Rachel mumbled from under many layers of quilts and blankets.

"I know," Kirsty agreed. "I'm cozy under the covers, but I feel like my nose and ears have frostbite."

"I kind of wish the heater was broken again," Rachel admitted, "so it would blast hot air everywhere."

"And so Michelle could magically pop out and surprise us," Kirsty said. Their new fairy adventure had started with the broken heater, just the day before.

It was the girls' first full day at the Winter Wonder Festival, and they knew the resort would have lots of fun activities scheduled. Rachel and Kirsty were excited to take part, but they also had plans of their own. They needed to find Michelle's

other two
magical
items!
Rachel
and Kirsty
had seen
how messy
winter weather

could get when Michelle's objects
were missing. Still, there was good
news. They had already tracked
down the magical snow globe. Now,
there would be plenty of snow for all
the outside fun. The girls could go
snowshoeing or sledding, and Mr. Tate
could go skiing.

However, Michelle's hat and candle
were still missing. Rachel and Kirsty
knew they would have to get them back

from Jack Frost's goblins soon. If they
didn't, no one could really enjoy all the
fun of the Winter Wonder Festival.

The girls got dressed as quickly as they
could, teeth chattering the whole
time. Then they rushed to the lodge
restaurant. They found an enormous
breakfast buffet there.

"Everything looks amazing," Rachel said.

"Yes, but I definitely don't want cold cereal or cold fruit. I need hot food!" Kirsty replied. "Waffles, pancakes, and scrambled eggs." She listed off the foods as she piled them on her plate.

"You should feel free to go outside," Devi said when she saw the girls. "There's lots of snow now. It started during your sleigh ride and came down all night. It's beautiful out there." But then Devi's smile fell. "If you do go out, though, you have to promise me you will bundle up. It's terribly cold." Devi looked very serious.

"We promise," Rachel said.

Kirsty glanced out the frosted window. The trees were bent over in the wind. "It looks pretty bad. Maybe we should

stay inside for a
while." Then she
dropped her voice
to a whisper,
so only Rachel
could hear. "We
can let the magic
come to us."

"There is a fun
craft project this
morning," Devi offered, pointing in the
direction of some tables in a room off
the lodge restaurant. A bunch of supplies
were piled in the middle of each. "And
there will be hot chocolate."

The girls smiled at each other. Their
minds were made up!

After breakfast, Rachel and Kirsty
joined the crafting table and began

making bird-seed ornaments. They listened to everyone passing by while they worked. No one wanted to go outside. They all wanted to sit by the fire.

Soon, Rachel and Kirsty wouldn't have a choice. Before long, they would have to brave the fierce wind and the brutal cold. They had to get that magic hat!

For the Birds

"I like the idea of helping the animals," Rachel said. She was using three different kinds of seeds to make a snowflake design on her ornament. Even though she was enjoying the craft, she kept looking outside. It still looked incredibly cold.

"We'll put them on the trees for all the birds," Kirsty said. "Devi was saying that deep snow drifts can make it hard for animals to find food."

"That makes sense. Many animals eat food from the ground," Rachel said. She looked around and noticed a group

of resort workers. They were gathered together and talking in hushed voices. They all looked worried. "Something is going on," Rachel said. "I'm going to figure out what it is."

Rachel picked up her mug and walked over to the hot chocolate stand. She stood as close as she could to the workers. She leaned toward them as she poured her drink.

"Not only that," a girl with thick raven-black hair said, "but none of the animals have their winter coats."

Lauren, who was in charge of the sleigh horses, shook her head. "The horses' hair is short and sleek, like it is in the middle of summer," she explained. "It's like their fluffy, warm coats disappeared."

"I saw a chickadee that was literally shaking in its nest," Alfonzo said. His blue eyes were sad.

Kirsty tried to hide her reaction. She didn't want the workers to know she had been listening. But the news was so tragic! She and Kirsty had to act quickly. Animals were in danger!

As soon as she returned to the craft table, Rachel told Kirsty what she had heard.

"That's horrible!" Kirsty agreed. "You think the missing hat is affecting the animals, too?"

"It sounds like it,"
Rachel said. "I hope the
deer and chipmunks
and other wild
creatures are OK."

"We can't wait
to find out,"
Kirsty insisted.
"We have to do
something."

"But it's dangerously cold out there.
Shouldn't we wait for the magic to come
to us?" Rachel asked.

"I think it just did," Kirsty said, smiling.
"Look at that window." Kirsty pointed.
There was a message etched in the frost
on the big picture window.

Join me, girls!

"It's Michelle!" Rachel exclaimed. "Let's go!"

Luckily, the girls had finished their projects and could quickly tidy up. Then they rushed to their room to grab their coats. "We need to tell my parents that we're going outside," Kirsty said, tossing her scarf over her shoulders.

The two friends found Kirsty's parents in their room. Mrs. Tate was sitting up in bed reading. She was wearing all of her outside winter clothes, including her coat and wool hat. Her fuzzy mittens made it hard to turn the pages of her book!

Mr. Tate was busy waxing his skis. "Are you going out?" he asked.

"We're going to hang our ornaments on a tree! For the birds!" Rachel answered with excitement. She held up her ornament. The pattern looked lovely as it spun around.

"Are you wearing long underwear?" Mrs. Tate asked, her forehead wrinkled with concern.

Kirsty nodded. "Two pairs."

"Don't forget your gloves," Mr. Tate added. "And come in before you're too cold."

The girls promised to be careful and then rushed to the lodge's lobby. Kirsty pulled her coat's zipper  tight under her chin and then pushed the heavy door open.

"I hope Michelle's still here," Rachel whispered.

"I sure am," a tiny, silvery voice declared.

But just as Rachel and Kirsty turned toward Michelle's voice, a gust of wind nearly blew them over. They stumbled back into the closed lodge door. The wind pressed against them, and tiny pieces of ice pricked their faces. The cold air swept into their lungs. The cold seemed to freeze them in place. They couldn't even move!

A Charm against the Chill

"I'm stuck," Kirsty mumbled through clenched teeth. "Frozen. Can't move."

"Oh no!" Michelle cried. "This is the work of Jack Frost, no doubt. Let me see if I can help you." She twirled her

73

wand in one hand. "I think I've got just the one! It will help you, but that won't affect the natural world," Michelle announced. The fairy took a deep breath, closed her eyes, and raised her wand.

When snowdrifts are high
And the temperature is low,
The winter's deep freeze
Causes nothing but woe.
The cold air still bites,
The snowflakes still flurry.
But remove the chill
From these girls in a hurry.

At once, Rachel could feel a warm glow inside her chest. It began to expand. As soon as she realized she could move again, she turned to look at Kirsty. Her best friend had a look of relief on her face.

"Phew!" Michelle
exclaimed. "I'm
so glad that
worked."
She glanced
around at
the trees, the
clouds, and the snow
on the ground. "The spell doesn't seem
to have affected anything else, so that's
good."

"That *is* a good thing," Rachel agreed.

"But it wouldn't be good if someone saw
you, Michelle." Kirsty glanced at the lodge.
She hoped no one was watching. "How
about you hide in my hood?" she suggested.

At once, the fairy flew over and landed
on Kirsty's shoulder. She then ducked
inside the soft hood of her coat.

"I can tell it's still super cold out here," Rachel said. "But I feel warm inside."

"That's how the spell is supposed to work," Michelle explained. "You should still be able to feel winter's chill, but you'll stay warm enough to be outside and get things done."

"Like hang up some ornaments," Rachel said.

"And track down some goblins," Kirsty said.

"And get back my hat," Michelle added. "Then everyone can enjoy being out here. Just look how beautiful it is."

Each girl placed her ornament on a tree branch, and then they took a moment to take in the wonder of winter. The sun had come out, and the snow gleamed in its golden light. Every tree branch was topped with a bright crust of snow. The air was fresh and crisp. Still, they knew that it was horribly cold. They were

lucky that they had the warmth of Michelle's special spell.

"Did you hear that?" Rachel whispered. "I thought I heard a voice."

The three friends did not speak, so they could pick up on any sounds. Everything was quiet, until there was a high-pitched giggle.

"It's too cold for anyone to be out here playing," Kirsty said. "The only people who have gone outside were the workers, and that's because they had to work."

"Those aren't people laughing," Michelle said. "That's the sound of goblins nearby! I bet they have my magic hat. That's why they can bear to be out in this cold."

"Well, they won't have your magic hat for long," Rachel declared. "Let's get it back!"

Gleeful Goblins

It was hard to move quietly through the snow. The top layer crunched when the girls put their boots through it. The snow was also very high in places. The girls grunted as they tried to pull their legs out of the deep holes.

The goblins' giggles were getting louder. "We must be close," Rachel whispered.

"Shhhh, you don't want them to hear you," Michelle reminded the girls.

Kirsty could tell there was a clearing up ahead. "It sounds like the goblins are on the other side of those trees." The three friends gathered together and peeked through a gap between the branches.

There was a large crew of goblins playing wintery games. The goblins were wearing hats, and gloves, and scarves, but not boots or long pants, even in the bitter cold. Michelle and the girls scanned the group. They did not see Michelle's magic hat, but they knew it must be close by.

Jack Frost's helpers all seemed to be having a blast. They were throwing

snowballs, making snow angels, and even building a snow fort!

The hat *had* to be on one of their green heads. There were hats of all styles and colors. Some were striped. Some had super-size pom-poms on top. One was extremely furry.

Just then, several goblins crawled out of the snow fort. One of them was wearing the cutest hat Kirsty had ever seen. "There it is!" she declared.

"I'm all roasty toasty!" the goblin wearing Michelle's hat declared. "This is the best hat ever!" Then the goblin began to dance a silly jig. He kicked up his feet, slinging clumps of snow through the air.

"Can I have the hat next?" one of the other goblins asked.

"Sure thing," the dancing goblin

replied. He took off Michelle's hat and handed it to the other goblin. "Just don't go far. We need to stay close together, so we can all stay warm."

"Did I mention that my hat allows everyone to enjoy the wonders of winter?" Michelle said with a little sigh. "I feel bad, but we have to take that hat back from him."

"But there are so many goblins around," Kirsty pointed out. "How will we get it back without being seen?"

"They're getting along so well," Rachel noted. "They aren't bickering like they usually do. Maybe we could reason with them."

Michelle shrugged her shoulders, her wings fluttering behind her. "We could give it a try." With that, she flew out

into the clearing,
and the girls
followed close
behind.

"Hello,
fellow fans
of winter,"
Michelle called
out, her voice full
of cheer. "Could we
speak with you for a
moment?"

At once, the goblins'
expressions changed from smiles to
frowns. "It's a silly fairy!" a goblin with
fuzzy mittens cried. "She's come to steal
the hat!"

"I'm not silly," Michelle said with a
smile. Her eyes sparkled with kindness.

"Don't listen to her! She'll put a spell on you!" warned a goblin with a long purple scarf.

"No," Michelle said. "Really, I won't."

"She'll steal our special hat!" yelled the goblin who was wearing the magic hat. "We won't be able to play outside!"

Michelle was usually a very patient fairy, but she had heard enough. "I am not going to steal *your* hat," she insisted, putting her hands on her hips. "I am going to get *my* hat back. Help me, girls!"

"They're after us!" yelled another goblin as he headed for the ski slopes. "Run! Get on the chairlift. Now!"

Before Kirsty or Rachel could do anything to help Michelle, the goblins scampered away.

Terrifying or Terrific?

The goblins ran down the path toward the ski slopes. Michelle and the girls watched as they piled their knobby green bodies onto the chairlift. Five goblins crammed themselves into just one seat!

Rachel and
Kirsty climbed
into the next
available chair
and pulled down
the safety bar.
"I can't watch,"
Kirsty said,
looking down.

"Are you afraid
of heights?" Michelle
asked.

"No, but I'm afraid a goblin is going
to fall," Kirsty admitted. "They aren't
following any of the ski lift rules."

"Don't worry," Michelle said. "I can
catch them with my wand, but it might
use all my magic if I do."

The chairlift carried them up the steep hillside. At the top, the goblins scrambled out and tumbled into one another. They turned into a huddle of sharp elbows and tight fists. "You fool!" one yelled. "They're right behind us!"

The girls leaped off the chairlift. Soon, they were hot on the trail of the goblins. "The one with your hat is at the front!" Rachel called to Michelle.

They saw a big red shed on the other side of the hilltop. Next to the shed was a line of inner tubes. Just below the tubes, there was a long, icy slope. Within the blink of an eye, goblins threw themselves on the tubes. They started to zoom down the hill, arms and legs poking out in every direction! They were all yelling.

"Yikes!"

"Ouch!"

"Noooooo!"

"Get off me!"

The girls ran up to the one inner tube
that was still at the top of the hill.

"That looks steep!" Kirsty said as she
looked down.

"That looks fun!" Rachel announced.

"It will be! Hop on!" Michelle directed.

As soon as the girls were safely on the tube, side by side, Rachel pushed off.

Kirsty gulped. Her stomach felt like it was still at the top of the hill, but they were flying down the slope at top speed.

"Wheeeeee!" Rachel yelled. A nervous giggle escaped from Kirsty's mouth. Up

ahead, the goblins' tubes were bumping into one another as if they were in a giant, snowy pinball machine.

"We're gaining on them!" Michelle said. They continued to pick up speed on the slippery ice.

"Wait! There's a fork in the path," Kirsty pointed out. Up ahead, a cluster of trees grew right in the middle of the trail. "Which way is the goblin with the hat going?"

The group of goblin tubes divided between the two paths. Michelle and the girls strained to catch a glimpse of the magic hat. "Hurry!" Michelle said. "We have to choose a path soon!"

"To the right!" Rachel shouted. "Go to the right!"

Kirsty and Rachel leaned all their weight to one side of the tube, and it slowly began to veer right. "We're going to hit the trees!" Kirsty warned.

Michelle raised her wand, and a stream of sparkles poured out and surrounded them. The tube whooshed to the right, barely missing a thick tree trunk.

"Thank you!" the girls replied together.

This path was narrow. It zigzagged around tree trunks and under low branches. The girls leaned from one side to the other, trying to guide the tube along the fast track. They could barely catch their breath! "Easy does it," Michelle advised from her perch on Rachel's hat. The fairy's wings whipped behind her with the changing wind.

"I can't see the goblins anymore," Rachel said. "Where are they?"

Just then, the friends' tube zipped out from the trees and into a meadow. Up ahead was a gigantic snowdrift. The mass of goblin tubes was headed straight for it!

"Watch out!" Rachel cried. "We're going to crash into the goblins!"

As the tubes hit the drift, the goblins slammed into the wall of snow. *Boom!* Green hands, feet, and heads stuck out of the frozen mound of white.

"Brrrrrrr!" the goblins all groaned. "It's freezing!"

"Did you hear that?" Michelle asked. "They said they're cold. That means the goblins don't have my hat anymore!" She lifted her wand and magically brought the girls' tube to a stop. Rachel and Kirsty jumped out and began sorting through all the hats, scarves, and gloves that had fallen off when the goblins hit the snowbank.

"I got it!" Kirsty called out, and she tossed the hat toward the fairy, who was hovering in midair.

Michelle twirled her wand, and a cloud of sparkles swirled around the adorable hat. The magic item shrunk to its Fairyland size, and Michelle held it tightly. "Once I take my magic hat back to Fairyland, everyone will be able to enjoy the outdoors again," Michelle said. Then she looked at the goblins. Some of them were still stuck in the snow. Others were shivering and knocking their knees together in the cold. "At least everyone is properly dressed for the cold weather," Michelle added with a wink.

Without another word,
Michelle vanished.
The girls
knew they
would see her
soon. They
still had one
more magic
item to find!
    Seeing the
chilly goblins, Rachel and Kirsty
decided to give them a hand. "I want to
go back to Jack Frost's Ice Castle." The
goblin with the fuzzy hat groaned as
Kirsty pulled him from the drift.

    "I know!" another goblin agreed as he
snatched a glove from Rachel. "The Ice
Castle is so much warmer! But Jack Frost
won't be happy that we lost the magic

hat." The goblins gathered together and stomped off, pouting.

Almost immediately, birds landed on nearby branches. The girls noticed squirrels trotting across the snow and a deer peeking out from the trees.

"It feels warmer already. The animals are coming out of their burrows again," Rachel said. "That's a good sign."

"I hope my parents venture out of their burrows soon, too," Kirsty said with a laugh. "That would be the best sign of all!"

The Longest Night

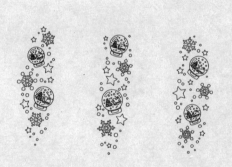

Contents

It Started with a Spark!

Kirsty reached for the lamp above her bedside table. "It's so dark in here. I can't even find the switch on the lamp," she mumbled. She and Rachel had just woken up. It was the morning of their last full day on Snowbound Island.

"I'll open the curtains," Rachel offered. She got out of bed and felt her way to the window in the dark. She tugged open the curtains, but no light came in. "That's weird," she said, staring out. "I wonder what time it is. It feels late in the morning, but it looks like the middle of the night."

"It's ten o'clock," Kirsty said, staring at her light-up watch. "So why is it pitch-black outside?"

At that moment, Rachel and Kirsty both realized what was happening.

"This is all because of Jack Frost," Rachel said.

"Yes," Kirsty added. "We still have to find the magical candle, or the nights will just keep getting longer and longer, and we'll barely see any sun."

In the two days they had been on Snowbound Island, the girls had encountered all kinds of magic. Most importantly, they had made a new magical friend. Michelle was the Winter Wonderland Fairy, and she was in charge of making sure everyone could enjoy the snowy season. Rachel and Kirsty had already helped her locate two of her missing magical items. Now, they just needed to track down one more, but they might need a flashlight to do it!

"I know that the days are shorter and the nights are longer in the winter," Kirsty said. "But why?"

"I'm not sure," Rachel answered. She plopped down on her bed and pulled the blankets around her. "But it's got to have something to do with the sun, right?"

As soon as Rachel said the word *sun*, a tiny light appeared. It had a golden glow, but it wasn't much larger than a speck of dust. The light floated in midair, between the two girls' beds. It seemed to grow brighter, and it made a humming sound.

"It must be some kind of fairy magic!" Kirsty said. The little spark looped around Kirsty's head, and then it swooped past Rachel's. It seemed to skip its way to the door.

"Quick! Put on your clothes!" Rachel insisted. "We need to follow it."

The girls had never dressed so quickly. "Don't forget extra layers," Kirsty advised. "With no sun, it will be extra cold."

When the girls opened the door, the spark flitted into the hallway. Even though it was daytime, the electric lights were still dim. Everything was quiet.

"It's like no one is awake," Rachel whispered. "Everyone must still be sleeping because there isn't any sun."

"But it's our last full day here!" Kirsty exclaimed. "I want my parents to have lots of fun. They can't just sleep all day! There's a snow hike and the campfire to celebrate the longest night. "

The hum of the tiny light grew louder.

"Don't worry, Kirsty," Rachel assured her friend. "We're both awake, and we're on the right track."

The girls followed the glowing, humming spark all the way through the lodge's silent lobby, out the front door, and along a snowy path. Not until they were safely hidden behind a pine tree did the glowing spark come to a stop. In an instant, the spark grew even brighter and bigger, and it became Michelle, the Winter Wonderland Fairy! She was still wearing her cozy winter coat and her darling hat with the tiny ears.

"Thanks for following me, girls," their new friend said. "I'm sorry I couldn't appear as myself earlier. My power is very weak. Showing up as a 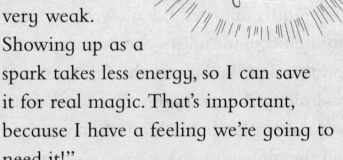 spark takes less energy, so I can save it for real magic. That's important, because I have a feeling we're going to need it!"

Away We Go

"It's almost lunchtime, and it's still dark out," Rachel said. "It seems so weird."

Kirsty and Rachel walked behind Michelle. The fairy flew with her wand high in the air, so it would light their way.

"In some parts of the world," Michelle explained, "there are only a couple of hours of sunlight in the winter. The places that are close to the poles have the shortest winter days."

"Why is that?" Kirsty asked.

"Well," Michelle began, "as Earth orbits the sun, it is tilted. One pole tilts toward the sun and the other pole away from the sun. The one that tilts toward the sun gets more of its energy—its light and heat—so it's summer there. It's winter in the one that is tilted away." The fairy paused to catch her breath. "Then, of course, six months later, the other pole is tilted toward the

sun," Michelle pointed out. "So they switch seasons."

Both girls nodded their heads.

"But that's science," Michelle said. "What's happening now is magic. We have to fix the magic so that science can do its job. Otherwise, everyone here will have winter and darkness forever!"

"At least it isn't as cold as yesterday," Kirsty said, trying to look on the bright side.

"Yes, you were both

amazing yesterday, and I have no doubt
you'll track down my magical candle,
too. It will be easy to find. It's in the
cutest snowflake lantern, and it's magic,
so it is always lit."

The girls nodded again, and the three
set off. They took the path down to
where they had seen the goblins the
day before, but this time there were no
goblins playing in the snow. Next, they
went to the barn. When they peeked
through the windows, they saw only the
horses and the sheep and the chickens.
"Shouldn't the barn be busy with
workers? They need to be getting ready
for the big festival tonight."

"I think people are still sleeping,"
Michelle said. "Winter is a fun time to
stay inside and snuggle, too." The fairy

closed her eyes and smiled at the cozy
thought.

"Except it's a big, important day!"
Kirsty insisted. "If people don't wake up
soon, they won't have any fun!"

Rachel knew what Kirsty was thinking.
Kirsty was worried about her parents.
She wanted them to enjoy their time

on the island! After all, Kirsty's mom had won the trip. Mrs. Tate's amazing painting of a winter scene had taken first prize in a contest.

"I'll bet this is going to be the log for the big campfire tonight," Rachel said. She pointed to a large tree that the workers had cut in the forest. "But they still need to trim it down and get it in to the fire ring. There's a lot to do!"

"This reminds me of one of King Oberon's favorite sayings," Michelle

began. "He always advises the young fairies. He tells us, 'You can only do what you can do.'"

Rachel and Kirsty looked at each other. King Oberon was married to Queen Titania. They were the kind, wise rulers of Fairyland. Sometimes, they spoke with grand words and fancy phrases that sounded like riddles, but both girls were certain they understood what Michelle had said.

"So, you're reminding us that we shouldn't worry about what we can't do," Rachel said.

"But that we *need* to do what we *can* do," Kirsty finished.

"Exactly," Michelle said. "And we *need* to find my beautiful candle in the snowflake lantern. Once we do that, everything will come into place."

"But it's so dark," Kirsty mumbled. "It's hard to believe there is light anywhere on the island."

"Kirsty!" Rachel exclaimed. "You're brilliant! The candle is not on the island at all. I'll bet the goblins took it back to Fairyland!"

A Frosty Fairyland

"You're absolutely right," Michelle said from her perch on Rachel's shoulder. "If it's dark here, it must also be dark in Fairyland. Jack Frost would want to keep the lantern close, so he could have the light in the Ice Castle."

Rachel and Kirsty thought this was good news, but Michelle did not look happy. Her wings drooped behind her, and she was nervously biting her lip. "Michelle, what's wrong?" Kirsty asked.

The fairy sighed. "My magic is getting weaker," she said. "I don't have enough power to get you to Fairyland, and I'm worried. What if I can't beat Jack Frost and his goblins on my own?"

"Don't worry, Michelle," Rachel said. "You won't get rid of us that easily. We have magic powder from Queen Titania."

"We carry it in our lockets, so we can travel to Fairyland anytime," Kirsty added. "You won't have to face Jack Frost or the goblins alone."

Even in the gloomy shadows, the girls could see Michelle's mood brighten. A smile spread across her face. "That's wonderful," the fairy said. "I'm ready whenever you are!"

The girls unzipped their winter coats. They dug under their warm scarves in search of their lockets. They had used the magic powder several times, but it always felt special . . . and a little scary. Soon, both Rachel and Kirsty had found and opened their lockets. "On the count

of three," Rachel
said. "One, two,
three!" The girls
took a pinch
of powder and
sprinkled it
over their heads.
At once, the air

filled with twinkling sparkles. Michelle
watched as a brisk wind wrapped around
the two friends. In only a moment, the
girls began to shrink to Fairyland size.
The wind grew stronger and lifted them
into the sky. Then *poof!* They were gone.

The three friends reappeared in
Fairyland. Now, Rachel and Kirsty
had shimmery wings on their backs.
Something else was different, too. In
Fairyland, near the Ice Castle, there was

light. Even though the skies were filled with a thick layer of gray clouds, there was a warm glow all around.

"Oh, it's light out!" Michelle exclaimed. "That must mean my magic candle and lantern are nearby."

"We've got to track them down," Rachel said. "It shouldn't be hard. It looks like the light is coming from over there."

"Yes, it's brighter on the other side of the Ice Castle," Kirsty said.

"Let's go," Michelle directed. "But be careful. We don't want them to know we're here."

The three fairies flapped their wings and flew toward the light. As they approached the Ice Castle, Michelle brought her finger to her lips. She wanted

to remind the girls to be quiet. Jack Frost
had goblin spies everywhere.

Rachel and Kirsty had been to the
Ice Castle before. The goblins often
stayed inside, and you could hear them
squabbling . . . or hear Jack Frost yelling.
Today, something special was happening.

Even from high above, it was clear that the goblins were not fighting. They were busy. They had set up work stations and were carrying supplies: wood, hammers, nails, and lights. They were building something!

"Look," Michelle said. "They're headed into the forest. It looks like they're taking everything up that hill."

Michelle and the girls followed the goblins into the woods. When they flew past, the local birds noticed them and chirped hello. "Shhhh," Michelle whispered, hoping the birds would help keep their secret.

As they neared the top of the hill, there was a clearing. Here, the air was full of the sounds of sawing and hammering. The hilltop was also bright with the most beautiful light.

"My candle and lantern!" Michelle said, pointing to an extra-tall pedestal with the lantern placed at the top. Inside the pretty lantern with snowflake cutouts was a thick candle. Its flame had a brilliant glow.

The pedestal was on a stage that the goblins were building. "How will we get

to the candle without the goblins seeing?"
Rachel wondered. "They're everywhere."

"Yes, but the pedestal is so tall, and
we're so fast, we can probably get it
before they even know we're here,"
Michelle said. Her eyes were full of hope,
but Kirsty and Rachel exchanged a
worried glance. They weren't so sure it
would be that easy!

Snowballs and Snowbirds

The three fairies sat on a snowy tree branch. They were about to set off to claim the candle. Their plan was to sweep in and out in secret, so the goblins wouldn't even know they had taken the candle from the top of the pedestal. "We need to hurry," Michelle advised. "My magic is almost gone. I need the candle back as soon as possible. So let's go—"

But before they could take off, a small flock of sweet snowbirds perched next to them. The birds landed with a fierce beating of their wings, and then they chirped, high and fast.

"Shhh," Michelle scolded. "We don't want the goblins to know we're here." Without a pause she grabbed Rachel and Kirsty by the hands. "Come on, girls!"

The snowbirds chirped even louder when the fairies took off. Kirsty glanced back, and she was almost certain that the birds were shaking their heads with concern.

Still, the fairies flew forward, aiming for the candle at the top of the pedestal. Michelle was in the lead. She sped like a dart toward her missing magic item. When she was almost in reach, she slammed to a stop in midair and bounced backward. *Whack.* The same happened to Rachel. And Kirsty. *Slam! Bam!*

"What was that?" Rachel wondered, shaking out her wings. Kirsty rubbed her sore head.

Michelle reached
forward and felt
something. She
placed her hands
flat and slid
them along an
invisible wall. "It's

a spell," she said. "It's a no-fairy force field.
We can't get to the pedestal." Michelle's
shoulders instantly slumped. "What do
we do now?" she wondered. Then a giant
snowball smacked into her side.

"Fairies!" a goblin screeched from
below.

"They're going to get the candle!"
another yelled.

"Snowball fight!" a third bellowed.

At once, snowballs came whizzing
at the fairies. All they could do was

dodge the sloppy balls of snow. But there were too many goblins and too many snowballs. Soon, the fairies were cold and soggy, their wings too wet to work.

"I can't keep flying," Kirsty yelled with concern. "My wings are too cold." She could feel herself drifting down.

"The fairies are falling!" a goblin called with excitement. "I'm going to catch one."

All three fairies tried to flap harder, but their wings only moved more slowly.

"This one is mine!" another goblin called, pointing a crooked finger.

"Mine! Mine! I want to give it to Jack Frost!" A long-eared goblin jumped up and swiped at Rachel's snow boot.

In an instant, the small flock of snowbirds swooped in. Three of the birds carefully

flew under the fairies. Rachel, Kirsty, and Michelle gratefully accepted their rides, holding on to the birds' soft neck feathers.

Three other birds flew up to the top of the pedestal and took hold of the lantern's handle. They weren't fairies, so they couldn't be stopped by the magical force field! They lifted the lantern, the candle still burning bright, high in the sky.

"Hit the candle! Knock out the flame!" one angry goblin demanded. "No one should have the light!" The goblins threw snowball after snowball, but none came close to the candle.

The red-beaked bird carrying Michelle knew just what to do. It flitted up toward the lantern. "Oh, thank you!" Michelle cried. The fairy reached out. As soon as she touched the lantern, there was a

brilliant burst of
golden light and
the dark winter
clouds cleared.

Safe on the
backs of the
snowbirds, Kirsty
and Rachel had an amazing view of
Fairyland from above. The winter sun
shimmered off the snow. Even Jack Frost's
Ice Castle glistened. King Oberon and
Queen Titania's palace shone like a
crystal jewel.

"Thank you so much, sweet
snowbirds!" Michelle cheered. "I should
have known you were trying to tell us
something. You knew there was an awful
spell around the pedestal, didn't you?"
The birds all chirped in reply. "Well,

Rachel, Kirsty, and I thank you from the bottom of our hearts."

The snowbirds found a sturdy nest and set down the young fairies. Michelle was anxious to return the candle to a safe place. "Thank you again, dear friends!" she called as the flock flew off. "And thank you, Kirsty and Rachel. It's time for me to get you back to Snowbound Island and all the fun you can share there." With a flash of her wand, the girls were far from Fairyland.

Snow Globe Spell

When Kirsty and Rachel arrived back
on Snowbound Island, it was bright out.
As usual, no time had passed while they
were gone. It was near noon by the
time they walked back to the lodge, and

everyone was outside getting ready for
the Solstice Celebration that night.

"I can't believe we slept in so late," one
worker said to another. "There's so much
to do."

"Can we help?" Rachel offered.

"No, but thank you," Devi replied. "You
should enjoy this day. It may be the
shortest of the year,
but it looks like
it might also be
the prettiest."

Kirsty took a
deep breath of
the crisp air and
felt the warmth
of the golden sun
of her face. The
snow sparkled.

"This really is a winter wonderland," Rachel said, her eyes squinting with cheer.

"Let's go find my parents. I don't want them to miss another second!" Kirsty said. She grabbed her friend's hand, and they began to run through the deep snow. They hadn't gone far when they heard their names.

"Kirsty! Rachel!"

They turned to see the Tates waving at them. They were standing near the lodge's gear rental shed. "We picked out snowshoes!" Mr. Tate called.

The girls rushed over. They were greeted with big hugs and a long list of plans for the afternoon.

"I can't imagine leaving without going ice-skating," Mrs. Tate said.

"And I'd love to go snow tubing, too," Mr. Tate added.

"Then, it sounds like there's something special tonight," Mrs. Tate said, squeezing her daughter's hand.

"Mom, thanks for bringing Rachel and me along on this trip," Kirsty said. "It's been amazing."

"Well, it's not over yet!" Mr. Tate insisted, closing the latch on his snowshoe. "Let's get out there."

Rachel and Kirsty enjoyed a long afternoon of wintery fun and adventure! By the time evening came, they were more than ready to sit down and relax in front of the lodge's outdoor fire.

The big log the girls had seen earlier in the day blazed in rich shades of yellow, red, and orange. The Tates and Rachel huddled together on benches around the fire. Rachel smiled and looked at her best friend. When something flickered in the corner of her eye, just past a cluster of pine trees, she had to ask, "Did you see that?"

"I did," Kirsty said. "Do you think it was a sign—for us?"

The girls left the fire and followed the flickering glow.

"Pssst, over here!"

They weren't surprised to find that the voice belonged to Michelle, who held her wand above her head like a searchlight. "Hello, friends," she said. "I wanted to

thank you for all of your help. Now, humans and fairies can really enjoy the wonders of winter. Just look at everyone!"

Kirsty and Rachel glanced back toward the fire. Kirsty saw her parents joyfully sipping hot chocolate. Some of the other guests were singing songs together. Everyone looked happy and cozy.

"We should thank you," Rachel said. "You've given us all kinds of fabulous winter memories."

"That's what I'm here for!" Michelle said. "Also, I wanted to give you these." She twirled her wand, and two rings magically appeared, floating in a milky cloud in midair. The rings both had tiny snow globes on them, with tiny silvery snowflakes inside.

"Oh, they're lovely,"
Kirsty said. The girls
each took a ring
and put it on.

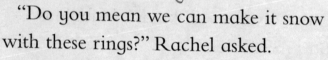

"They are
good for one
special snowfall,
as a gift from
me," Michelle
said.

"Do you mean we can make it snow
with these rings?" Rachel asked.

"Yes, just twist off the top, shake it,
and then you'll have snow," Michelle
explained.

"But it's so beautiful. I don't ever want
to empty the snow," Kirsty said. "After this
weekend, I think I want to trust nature
with all the weather and the seasons."

"I agree," Rachel said. "And I'll also trust our fairy friends."

Michelle looked very serious all of a sudden. "Your trust means a lot," the fairy said. "Thank you for being such amazing friends to the fairies. I'll look forward to seeing you again." She blew glittery kisses toward the girls and disappeared in a flurry of snowflakes.

Rachel and Kirsty pulled their mittens back on over their special snow globe rings. They linked arms and headed back to the fire where everyone was having a merry time. "It's the longest night of the year," Kirsty whispered.

"Yes," Rachel replied, "and I'm glad I get to spend every bit of it with you."

Now that they had helped Michelle find her magic candle and snowflake lantern,

things would return to normal. The days
would slowly get longer and the nights
shorter. After a while, with more sunlight,
the season would turn to spring. Then
flowers would start to bud, and the snow
would finally melt. But that was months
away. Rachel and Kirsty still had lots of
wonderful winter days and cozy winter
nights to share together before then.

THE Friendship FAIRIES

Rachel and Kirsty have found all of
Michelle's missing magic items.
Now it's time for them to help

Esther
the Kindness Fairy!

Join their next adventure in this
special sneak peek . . .

The Start of Summer

"It's so amazing to be back on Rainspell Island again—*together!*" said Kirsty Tate, leaning out her window and taking a deep breath of sea air.

Her best friend, Rachel Walker, clapped her hands and bounced up and down on her tiptoes.

"Today is the start of the most amazing summer vacation *ever*," she said. "I'm sure of it!"

They were sharing a room at the Sunny Days Bed & Breakfast on the island where they had first met and become best friends. They were so happy to be there again on vacation together. The girls shared a quick hug before rushing down the narrow stairs to the cozy breakfast room. Their parents were already there, poring over leaflets about activities on the island.

"I'm sure we can find some new things to do," said Mr. Walker, "even though we have visited this island so many times before."

"How about a nice long hike?" suggested Mr. Tate as the girls slipped

into their seats and poured some cereal.
"It'd be interesting to explore more of the
island—we all love seeing its beautiful
plants and trees."

Rachel and Kirsty shared a smile. They
had an extra-special secret reason why
they loved Rainspell Island so much.
It was here that they had first become
friends with the fairies!

"Hiking would be a great start to the
trip," said Mr. Walker. "Let's head out
after breakfast, shall we?"

"Here's something interesting," said Mrs.
Walker, holding out a bright yellow flyer.
"It's called the Summer Friends Camp."

Rachel took the flyer and read out loud.
"'A day camp for children staying on the
island. Make new friends and join in lots
of fun activities.' It sounds awesome!"

As Kirsty and Rachel were looking at the flyer and chattering about the activities, the breakfast-room door opened and Mr. Holliday came in. He ran the bed and breakfast, and he glanced at the flyer as he put some toast down on the table.

"My daughter Ginny's helping run that camp with her best friend, Jen," he said.

Kirsty and Rachel exchanged a special smile, wondering if Ginny and Jen's friendship was as strong as theirs. They knew that they were lucky to have each other.

"Is it OK if we go to the Summer Friends Camp instead of going on the hike?" Kirsty asked. "It sounds like lots of fun."

"Of course," said Mr. Tate. "We'll see you later. You can tell us all about it!"

"The Summer Friends Camp is held at Rainspell Park," said Mr. Holliday. "I'm sure you'll have a wonderful time."

When they had finished breakfast, the Tates and the Walkers put on their backpacks and hiking boots and set out on their hike. Rachel and Kirsty waved good-bye and then headed off toward Rainspell Park. The bed and breakfast was on a tree-lined road that overlooked the ocean, and as they walked along they saw the ferry heading toward the island.

"Remember when we met on the ferry that first day?" Rachel asked, smiling at her best friend. "That was one of the best days of my life."

"Mine, too," said Kirsty. "Everything I do is more fun now that I have you to share it with—including our fairy adventures!"

The girls held hands and smiled when they saw that they were both wearing the friendship bracelets that Florence the Friendship Fairy had given them. Rainspell Island was the place where the girls had first made friends with the fairies, so it had a very special place in their hearts.

"I hope we'll meet some more fairies while we're here," said Rachel. "I love making new fairy friends."

"Fingers crossed we'll make some new human friends, too," Kirsty added. "The Summer Friends Camp sounds like such a fun idea."

They reached the entrance to Rainspell Park and walked through the open gates,

gazing around at colorful flowerbeds
and huge old trees. The wide gravel paths
were dotted with benches, and a large
fountain was bubbling and splashing
beside the bandstand.

"Look," said Rachel, "there's a sign for
the camp."

A bright yellow sign pointed them
past the fountain and around a bend.
They saw a large tepee-style tent in the
middle of the grass. It was surrounded
by colorful balloons, and the sign next to
the tent said, *Welcome to the Summer
Friends Camp!*

Still holding hands, Rachel and
Kirsty walked into the tent. It was
cool inside, and decorated with rainbow-
colored silk. A smiling teenage girl

hurried to greet them. She was wearing a mint-green name tag that said, *Jen*, decorated with delicate, dark-gray birds.

"Welcome to our camp," she said. "Come and join us!"

Be sure to read all the books in the FRIENDSHIP FAIRIES series!

RAINBOW magic

Which Magical Fairies Have You Met?

- ☑ The Rainbow Fairies
- ☐ The Weather Fairies
- ☐ The Jewel Fairies
- ☐ The Pet Fairies
- ☐ The Sports Fairies
- ☐ The Ocean Fairies
- ☐ The Princess Fairies
- ☐ The Superstar Fairies
- ☐ The Fashion Fairies
- ☐ The Sugar & Spice Fairies
- ☐ The Earth Fairies
- ☐ The Magical Crafts Fairies
- ☐ The Baby Animal Rescue Fairies
- ☐ The Fairy Tale Fairies
- ☐ The School Day Fairies
- ☐ The Storybook Fairies
- ☑ The Friendship Fairies

SPECIAL EDITION

Which Magical Fairies Have You Met?

- ❏ Joy the Summer Vacation Fairy
- ❏ Holly the Christmas Fairy
- ❏ Kylie the Carnival Fairy
- ❏ Stella the Star Fairy
- ❏ Shannon the Ocean Fairy
- ❏ Trixie the Halloween Fairy
- ❏ Gabriella the Snow Kingdom Fairy
- ❏ Juliet the Valentine Fairy
- ❏ Mia the Bridesmaid Fairy
- ❏ Flora the Dress-Up Fairy
- ❏ Paige the Christmas Play Fairy
- ❏ Emma the Easter Fairy
- ❏ Cara the Camp Fairy
- ❏ Destiny the Rock Star Fairy
- ❏ Belle the Birthday Fairy
- ❏ Olympia the Games Fairy
- ❏ Selena the Sleepover Fairy

- ❏ Cheryl the Christmas Tree Fairy
- ❏ Florence the Friendship Fairy
- ❏ Lindsay the Luck Fairy
- ❏ Brianna the Tooth Fairy
- ❏ Autumn the Falling Leaves Fairy
- ❏ Keira the Movie Star Fairy
- ❏ Addison the April Fool's Day Fairy
- ❏ Bailey the Babysitter Fairy
- ❏ Natalie the Christmas Stocking Fairy
- ❏ Lila and Myla the Twins Fairies
- ❏ Chelsea the Congratulations Fairy
- ❏ Carly the School Fairy
- ❏ Angelica the Angel Fairy
- ❏ Blossom the Flower Girl Fairy
- ❏ Skyler the Fireworks Fairy
- ❏ Giselle the Christmas Ballet Fairy
- ❏ Alicia the Snow Queen Fairy

📖 SCHOLASTIC

Find all of your favorite fairy friends at
scholastic.com/rainbowmagic

3 stories in each one!